BY

# ANDREW T. PELLETIER

The Toy Farmer

PICTURES BY

## SCOTT NASH

Dutton Children's Books

*With special thanks to Scott Whitehouse*
*for his Photoshop design work.*

DUTTON CHILDREN'S BOOKS
A division of Penguin Young Readers Group

Published by the Penguin Group
Penguin Group (USA) Inc., 375 Hudson Street, New York, New York 10014, U.S.A.
Penguin Group (Canada), 90 Eglinton Avenue East, Suite 700, Toronto, Ontario, Canada M4P 2Y3
(a division of Pearson Penguin Canada Inc.) • Penguin Books Ltd, 80 Strand, London WC2R 0RL, England
Penguin Ireland, 25 St Stephen's Green, Dublin 2, Ireland (a division of Penguin Books Ltd) • Penguin Group
(Australia), 250 Camberwell Road, Camberwell, Victoria 3124, Australia (a division of Pearson Australia Group
Pty Ltd) • Penguin Books India Pvt Ltd, 11 Community Centre, Panchsheel Park, New Delhi - 110 017, India
Penguin Group (NZ), 67 Apollo Drive, Mairangi Bay, Auckland 1311, New Zealand (a division of
Pearson New Zealand Ltd) • Penguin Books (South Africa) (Pty) Ltd, 24 Sturdee Avenue, Rosebank,
Johannesburg 2196, South Africa • Penguin Books Ltd, Registered Offices:
80 Strand, London WC2R 0RL, England

*Library of Congress Cataloging-in-Publication Data*

Pelletier, Andrew Thomas.
The toy farmer / by Andrew T. Pelletier; illustrated by Scott Nash.—1st ed.
p. cm.
Summary: A toy farmer on a tractor that Jed finds in
the attic transforms his bedroom into a real farm,
where a vine grows and produces one enormous pumpkin.
ISBN: 978-0-525-47649-8 (hardcover)
[1. Agriculture—Fiction. 2. Toys—Fiction. 3. Magic—Fiction.]
I. Nash, Scott, date, ill. II. Title.
PZ7.P3639Toy 2007   [E]—dc22   2006024779

Published in the United States by Dutton Children's Books,
a division of Penguin Young Readers Group
345 Hudson Street, New York, New York 10014
www.penguin.com/youngreaders
Designed by Sara Reynolds and Abby Kuperstock

Manufactured in China
First Edition
3  5  7  9  10  8  6  4  2

One day, while he was poking around in the darkest back corner of the attic, Jed discovered an old wooden box. The only thing inside the box was a bright red toy tractor. At the wheel sat a farmer, wearing a plaid shirt and a straw hat with a wide brim.

When Jed showed the toy to his dad, his dad said, "I *wondered* where that old thing had gone off to!" It turned out that it had been *his* toy, way back when he was Jed's age.

"Craziest toy I ever had!" he told Jed. His dad wore a secret little smile and winked at Jed as if he knew something that he wasn't telling. Jed wanted to know more, but his dad just kept on grinning.

"Let's just say that's *some* farmer!" was all he said.

Jed had fun with his new toy. He drove it around and around on the thick green rug in his room, pretending that he was plowing and planting and harvesting.

That night before Jed climbed into bed, he parked the tractor
right at the edge of the rug. He bent down close to the farmer.
"We'll get back to work, first thing tomorrow!" he whispered.

Jed awoke to the low, rumbling sound of an engine, coming from quite close by. He threw his feet over the edge of the bed, and, to his surprise, they landed *not* on the green rug but in deep, soft dirt. Overnight his rug had been replaced by a neat square field. And the red tractor was plowing it. The Toy Farmer looked up and waved his straw hat.

"Mornin'!" he called.

"Mornin'!" replied Jed. It was all he could think of to say.

The farmer went on working as if nothing had happened. But Jed knew dirt when he saw it, and his green rug had *definitely* disappeared.

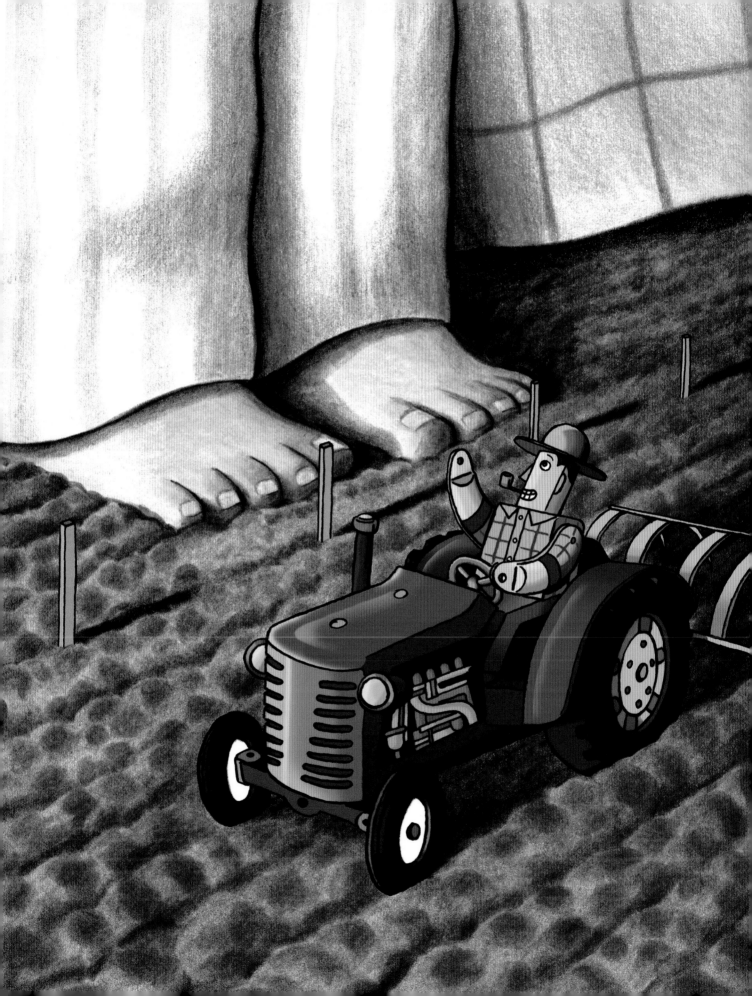

The next day the tractor was rumbling round and round the neat square field.

Day after day, the Toy Farmer was very busy. Sometimes he was tilling. Other times he was weeding.

"Mornin'!" the farmer always said.

"Mornin'!" Jed always replied.

When Jed noticed that a tiny green sprout had popped up in the middle of the field, he asked, "What's that you're growing?"

"You'll see," replied the Toy Farmer.

Each day the sprout was a bit taller. Leaves began to spring out from its stem, and little green vines curled out over the dirt.

The plant grew and grew. Its leaves and vines spread over the ground and grew crazily up the walls and over the windows.

The plant grew and grew. Once in a while Jed spied the Toy Farmer driving his tractor around in the shade of the broad green leaves. Sometimes he heard the farmer singing "Blue Moon of Kentucky," and he liked to join right in. The giant plant swayed in time to the tune.

A yellow blossom appeared on the thick main stem. It was as big around as a garbage can lid. Jed was sad when the flower shriveled and fell off. But he noticed that where the blossom had been there was now a tiny green fruit, barely bigger than his thumb.

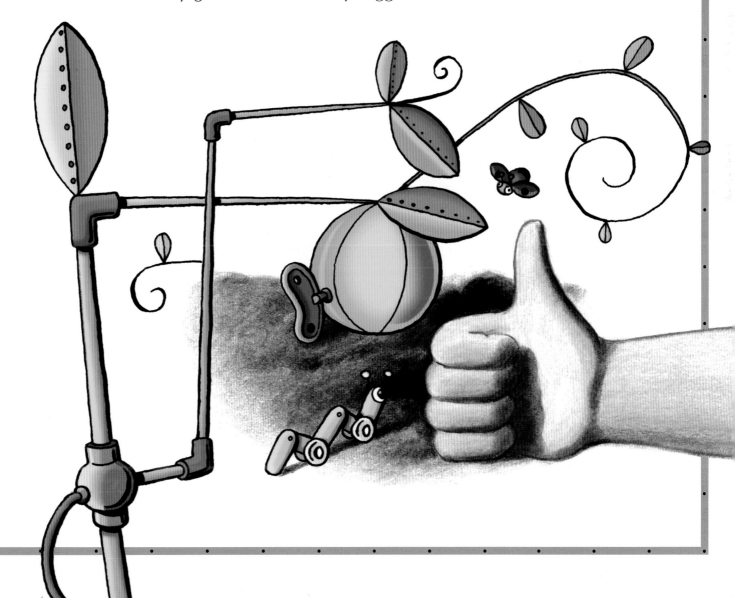

The little green fruit began to grow. One day it was as big as a baseball. The next it was as big as a basketball. Each morning it seemed to Jed that it was twice as large as when he had last looked. In no time it was as fat as a truck tire, and still it grew. By now, Jed and the Toy Farmer had to water it with a garden hose. And still it grew.

Then, right when the humongous thing was beginning to bulge against the walls and windows of Jed's bedroom, it began to change color. At first Jed noticed just the barest hint of yellow, right near the stem. The yellow spread down the wide sides, and then slowly the entire, gigantic thing turned a bright, bright orange.

Jed was the owner of the biggest pumpkin that anyone had ever seen.

When word of Jed's giant pumpkin spread, folks came running from miles around just to look in the window and stare. They all asked Jed how he had grown such a thing, but Jed just flashed a secret little smile, one that said he knew something he wasn't telling.

Somebody suggested to Jed that he should take his pumpkin down to the county fair and enter it in the giant pumpkin contest.

There was just one little problem: how was he supposed to get the gigantic thing out of his bedroom? Luckily, the Toy Farmer had a saw handy, and together he and Jed took the side of the room clean off. After that, Jed sawed through the stem, and then he and the Toy Farmer rolled the pumpkin right out of his bedroom onto the back of a big truck.

People lined the roads for miles just to watch Jed's pumpkin make its way to the fair. They cheered and waved and shouted "Good luck!" Jed rode on top of his pumpkin and waved back and sang "Blue Moon of Kentucky" at the top of his lungs.

The judges at the fair took one look, and all agreed they couldn't remember the last time they had seen anything like Jed's pumpkin.

"Astounding!" said the first judge.

"Incredible!" cried the second judge.

"No ordinary prize will do!" shouted the third.

Instead of the usual blue ribbon, they awarded Jed's pumpkin a special blue ribbon, ten times longer and five times wider than a regular ribbon. The ribbon had Jed's name on it, and it spelled out "GRAND CHAMPION" in big bold letters.

The judges were so impressed with Jed's pumpkin that they asked him if they could borrow it for Halloween. "It'll make the biggest jack-o'-lantern the county has ever seen!" they said. "We'll shoot car headlights through the eyes and mouth and scare everyone for miles around!" Jed thought it was a great idea.

It was his proudest moment. But then Jed remembered he had someone else to thank.

He rushed home and into his bedroom to share the special ribbon with the Toy Farmer. But while he was away at the fair, all of the leaves and vines and dirt had been swept away, and his room was back to normal. It looked as if nothing at all had happened. And the Toy Farmer was nowhere to be found.

Jed just sat down in the middle of his green rug. He missed the Toy Farmer terribly. He was so blue that he skipped supper.

When Jed's dad came up to check on him and saw his sad, lonely face, he knew exactly what was wrong.

He took Jed up to the attic and opened another old box, one that Jed hadn't noticed before. He pulled out a faded blue ribbon, exactly as long and exactly as wide as Jed's. This ribbon had his dad's name written on it, and it, too, spelled out "GRAND CHAMPION" in big bold letters.

"Don't worry," his dad told Jed. "That Toy Farmer will show up again. He always does!"